The Light Gets Darker

Richard Dale

Dear Claire,

So lovely to meet you,
and even better now I'm in
the light. Lots of love
                    Richard Dale
                    June '21

DEDICATION

For all those on the journey out of darkness

.

CONTENTS

ACKNOWLEDGMENTS

I would like to thank all those who've helped me to wake up, and who continue to support me on my exciting new journey towards freedom and light.

FORWARD

I love my family very much, and I would never want to do anything to knowingly hurt them, but as many readers of this book will know, when you've left a high control religion, which shows many signs of being a cult, you have to accept that your family members who remain within it will view you saying anything about your past life within that religion as malicious. Despite the fact that they might spend many hours preaching about their religion and giving out literature that openly criticizes other religions, they will not tolerate those who say anything negative about their religion.

I am not writing this book simply to criticize a religion, but hope that what I write might be helpful to those who are recovering from being in such a religion, or perhaps are still within one and are starting to question some of the teachings or practices. I have no desire to disturb those who are very happy within their religion. However, from my own experience I know how hard it was to come to terms with the gradual realization that what I had believed so sincerely for so long was not completely trustworthy, and that some aspects of it were decidedly harmful.

My personal experience relates to over 30 years as a member of the religious group known as Jehovah's Witnesses, as well my gradual waking up and subsequent exit from the religion. Most of the chapters in this book will have particular relevance to those who've also had a connection with this religion, but I've tried to minimize the very specific terms related to Jehovah's Witnesses so that the content may also resonate with those who've experienced similar things, but in different contexts. While speaking about specific religious terminology, let me say that while I was one of Jehovah's Witnesses, I served as an elder, a substitute circuit overseer, and as a regular pioneer. In ordinary language, that means I spent many hours every week going from house to house to spread the word.

I've been writing quite a lot of short stories and even imaginary magazine study articles that might appear if the long promised light ever did get switched on. I've included several of these stories and the final two chapters contain two of the aforementioned study articles. These articles will have less meaning to those unacquainted with the format of the study materials used by Jehovah's Witnesses. However, for those who did spend many years attending such religious meetings, I hope that these articles will provide a glimpse of what such material could look like in a better future. They do attempt, quite seriously, to provide a scriptural basis for the radical changes suggested within the articles. These articles are completely fictitious and satirical, and in no way are intended to reflect the viewpoint of Jehovah's Witnesses or any of their associated corporations. The Bible references are from the New International Version, as this translation permits the fair use of its content in works such as this one. However, you may wish to check the scriptures in the translation of the Bible that you are familiar with.

The journey out of darkness and towards freedom and light is a long one for most people, and could lead them to atheism, agnosticism, another religion, or simply a very personal spirituality. I still consider myself at the beginning of this journey, and if I do go on to write further books on this topic, I expect the next stages of my personal journey to inform what I write in the future.

I am so grateful to the many friends who support me in my new life. Some of these friends I shunned for many years because I believed that was the loving thing to do to them. My love and appreciation for these individuals knows no bounds!

The light got darker and darker until one day I mustered up the courage to open the door and get out.

1 THE FATHER

By now, Thomas, the eldest son, had been living and working in Northampton for 3 years and only got back home every few weeks.

At the end of November, his mother had told him that his father was not well and had been for some tests. Neither mother nor father were often ill, the mother least of all, and that was only for really serious illness. In fact, the only time anyone could remember her being ill was when she was struck with meningitis. It was really serious at the time, and rather upsetting for Thomas and his sister Lydia, the third child, as they were both in Venice when they got the news that she'd been rushed to hospital. The father did get flu occasionally, and on some of those occasions he even missed out on his nightly visits to the pub.

There was something ominous in this latest

news; there was mention of coughing up blood. Thomas called home more frequently in the next few days as results of the tests were anticipated.

Communication between father and son had never really been possible, but this latest development brought a softening to their relationship. Thomas dreaded his father answering the telephone when he called, and the pressure he'd feel to make conversation, even though his father tended to use complete words on the phone, so it was easier than face-to-face contact. Throughout their childhood, the children rarely elicited more than a sort of grunt from their father. There were many different tones, and it wasn't an unfriendly grunt. It's similar to the sound you might make if you try to imitate a cow, but not the moo part of it. Sometimes, when the mother would tell Thomas to go and show his father a picture he'd done at school, the father would make his standard noise, and the mother would urge him to show more interest, and the next noise would then be considerably higher in tone.

Suddenly, the illness gave Thomas something real to talk about, and the father reciprocated with actual comments about how he was feeling and news about the test results not having been returned yet.

It wasn't long before lung cancer was diagnosed, and this was particularly tragic as the father had finally succeeded in giving up smoking two years earlier.

He then went through several months of chemotherapy and radiotherapy, but with words like 'aggressive' and 'secondary' being heard at each follow-up appointment, things did not look good.

In some ways, it was a special time for the mother and father. Theirs was a marriage in which nothing ever seemed likely to break them up, but the personal time they spent together had become extremely minimal. The two things that stretched the marriage to breaking point were the mother's change of religion, around the time that the 5th child was born, and the father's drinking, which had intensified a little before that. As the mother moved further and further towards the religion, so the father drank more, and as the father drank more, so the mother clung to the religion. One of the reasons the mother devoted herself so intensely to her new religion was because of the worries she felt about having an alcoholic husband and the strains of raising children, and the father, in his turn, felt that he was losing his family to religion and so drank more than ever. He was so opposed to the religion that when he was drunk, he even burnt some of her books. Within her religion, this sort behaviour from a husband is viewed as religious persecution and that leads to an even greater need to show loyalty to the religion over all else.

Incredibly, the marriage had survived. There was only one time in all those years that the mother had tearfully crept into her eldest son's room and said she thought she might have to leave the father, and take all the children with her. But she didn't.

The religion made communication with the father difficult for all the children. One by one they had all followed the mother into the religion and the father was even more isolated as a consequence.

The father continued to work through those months and yet was only able to do so because of his wife's support. A few weeks in and he couldn't dress himself without her help. A few more weeks, and a tumour had been found in his brain so that he couldn't walk without her going ahead of him, and with his hand resting upon her shoulder. In those six months they almost returned to the days of their courtship. They would go out for lunch together, visit garden centres, and he totally stopped drinking. And, whereas the mother had spent the previous 17 years engaged in some form of religious activity on most days, now she was devoted to the care of her husband, and a determination to get him well again.

The mother is known for her eternal optimism, and never was it more evident than in her confidence that he would get better.

One Monday morning in May, Thomas had a sudden feeling that he should drive home. His mother had told him that the father was not too bad, and had still been at work until the previous Monday, but because he was still in some pain, the doctor had decided he would be better off having a few days in the hospital, to be monitored and to have some tests. Thomas drove straight to the hospital, arriving around lunchtime, and was surprised not to see his mother's car in the car park, or the cars of any of his siblings. He was too scared to go in. It's hard to say whether he was more fearful of having to speak to his father or of being greeted with bad news, but he avoided both possibilities and drove to the family home instead. He let himself in, and as he suspected when he saw the empty driveway, there was no one at home.

These were the early days of mobile phones, but he did finally manage to get hold of his sister, Lydia. She told him that she and their mother would be home soon. He waited. He showed no negative reaction when they told him they'd spent the morning in the preaching activity of the religion. He was in no place to criticize whatever they were doing; they were there the whole time, dealing with the father's illness, and he was just there every few weeks. The mother and his sister were delighted to see him and they all had lunch together. It was about half past three before he felt able to gently mention that it might be nice to get up to the hospital to see Dad. They said they were planning to go in at some point that afternoon, but with the mother having provided such constant care, she wanted to make the most of this time while he was in the hospital.

When they arrived at his bedside, he was very

sedated, almost to the point that it wasn't clear that he knew who was there. There were moments of brief lucidity, and in those moments they all took turns squeezing his hand and saying reassuring things about what the hospital were trying to do for him. At some point, the doctor assigned to the father's care asked to have a word. She was quite matter of fact, but looking back, it was because she was speaking in a way that reflected the obviousness of the situation.

After this conversation, the three of them went back out to the car to talk about it. The mother repeated the doctor's words, and was as much upset with the doctor's bluntness, as she was knocked sideways by the implication of the words:

"We'd like to move him to the bigger hospital to run some more tests, but we're worried that if we move him, he might finish his days there."

For the first time, at least openly, the mother started crying. This was the very first moment she had considered the possibility that he might actually die.

They went back inside and agreed that it would be good to move him, to see what else could be done. Thomas suggested that the other children should be told, and they were. Within an hour, the father, in his bed, was wheeled into the ambulance ready for the journey to the big hospital. The mother turned as if to travel with Thomas and Lydia, but at their urging, she was persuaded to travel with her husband in the ambulance.

At the next hospital, the situation worsened. All the children were there now, and it was decided to call the father's siblings. No one really found out for sure if any tests were done. The father was wheeled out at one point and wheeled back in again, but that seemed more of a response to one of the aunts shouting at a doctor:

"Bloody do something! Can't you see my brother's dying?"

The father lost all consciousness about an hour later, and the intervals between his breaths became longer and longer. Everyone was in a big circle around the bed, and people continued to take turns holding his hand. At one point, Matthew, the fourth child, started to cry, and one of the aunts quickly reprimanded him:

"Stop that, Matthew! Your father wouldn't want that."

One of the intervals seemed to go on for about 6 minutes and then another breath came. This led to someone repeating what one of the doctors had said earlier:

"He's an incredible fighter, your father."

Then there was another really long interval, but no one dared to conclude that this was the last one. A small tear slowly made it's way down the mother's cheek.

And everyone knew.

2 HAPPINESS

Thomas had clung to his mother all his life, and so much was his enthusiasm for everything she stood for, that she even felt he'd motivated and driven her on in much of what she'd done.

20 years after his death, Thomas now reflected back on the very few moments in which he felt he'd connected his father. In fact, perhaps it was only at the moment of his death that his real journey to understand him began.

Thomas was 8 years old when he first saw anything to do with the religion that he and his mother would go on to join. A man and woman were standing at the front door presenting his mother with a book. Thomas and his three siblings were very shy, and the fifth was still to be born. He remembers sneaking a view of the couple as he stood behind a wall at the foot of the stairs. He has no memory of what they said, but he will always remember the book that came into the house that day. The cover of the book was gold, and the title was 'Happiness'. As the months and years passed, it was almost irrelevant what the religion taught, as just the existence of a golden book about happiness was enough to capture his attention, and ultimately his devotion. His love for his mother played a significant role too.

His father detested the religion right from the very start, and that somehow seemed silly to Thomas who trusted his mother's judgment in everything. The only thing that he had thus far connected with his father on was Ken Dodd[1]. His father was uncontrollable with laughter in the theatre when he'd taken them all to see him in Wolverhampton, and Thomas reacted similarly. He was also deeply moved by Ken Dodd's song about happiness[2], and forever connected his own happiness with the sentiments of that song and the laughter he started experiencing that day. Sadly, the father didn't laugh much at home, and as the religion featured more and more strongly, his laughter vanished.

The mother had always explained away the

---

[1] Ken Dodd was a British comedian and singer, and famed for his incredibly long stages shows.
[2] Happiness' is a song written by American country musician Bill Anderson, and performed by Ken Dodd and released on EMI's Columbia Label in 1964.

father's animosity towards the religion by saying that in the father's family there'd been a lot of upset caused when his mother had 'gone potty', as they described it in those days, and had gone after some American religion and given away lots of money. No one ever said what type of mental health issues the grandmother was dealing with, and neither was it ever specified which religion she'd gone after. However, several years later, when the grandmother had died and the old family farmhouse was being sold, his father and his father's siblings were all given a chance to go over the house and choose items they would like. Each family group was given a sheet of stickers. The stickers that Thomas's family had were actually just plain white circles with a star drawn on each one in blue ink. They roamed the house, but found that most of the best bits had several stickers on them already. Thomas ended up with a little china dog.

The house is enormous and they saw parts of it that day that they'd never seen before, or since. Then, in the attic, they came upon something remarkable. A small bookcase filled with books that seemed to have stood undisturbed for decades. It had evidently been carried up there and reassembled with all the books, just as it once must have looked in one of the main rooms of the house. As Thomas, Alison, Lydia, and their mother approached the bookcase, they couldn't quite believe their eyes. All of the books were old publications of their very own religion. It was a mystery and knowing how much the father and his siblings, their aunts and uncles, hated the religion of Thomas's mother, no one dared to ask anything about the books. Stickers were placed on the bookcase and in due course it did arrive in the family home. In the quiet discussions that took place between mother and son, the mother suggested that perhaps their grandfather had taken an interest in the religion at some point in the past. He had died long before any of the children were born.

All these years later, Thomas wonders whether the very religion his grandmother had 'gone after' and for which his father had such an aversion, was the very same religion that they had joined.

Another memory came back to Thomas: A moment from childhood in which he had really felt happy at the idea of trying to connect with his father. He'd come in from school and his mother was next door, setting the old lady's hair. The doorbell rang and he went to answer it. Two men stood there, and a large truck stood on the drive. They pointed to the large puddle of water in the middle of the drive and said that the whole drive could do with being resurfaced. When it had rained heavily, it was necessary to leap from the car in order to avoid a shoeful of water. The two men went on to explain that they had been doing some road repairs at the top of the village and they had enough supplies to redo this drive. Thomas ran to get some paper and carefully noted all the details down. He assured them that he thought his parents would be very interested and that they'd get back to them soon.

When the mother came home, Thomas was eager to tell her all about it, and she agreed that it did seem like a great offer. She suggested that he should tell his father about it after dinner. Thomas said he didn't feel able to tell him, so asked her to do it. He kept pestering her and finally she did. He hid behind the wall leading into the living room. She explained it exactly as Thomas had told her to and he was pleased at how she put it. She handed the father the piece of paper. Thomas was nervously hopeful, and felt quite excited as he stood in the passageway listening. The father took one glance at the paper and replied in two words:

"Bloody pikeys[3]!"

The disappointment Thomas felt and the distance these words created between him and his father lasted for many years.

It is only now, as Thomas has woken up to the realities of the religion he'd fallen in love with when he saw that golden book 38 years earlier, that he's starting to piece together his father, and all that he'd really stood for.

He thought back to the memorial service that had been held for his father, and the more than 300

---

[3] Pikeys is an offensive term for gypsies, travellers or Roma.

people who attended. He thought of the couple that came up to him at that service and told him how much they appreciated what his father had done for them. Thomas had no idea of any such things. He heard of financial assistance his father had given, he heard of great wisdom he had shared, and he heard of the life he lived in the pub every night. He heard how everyone in the pub used to watch the door around the time that Thomas's father would arrive, excitedly anticipating his entrance. He remembered back to a family wedding and the laughter of everyone in the marquee, not laughing because of the speech being given, but because of the asides his father was shouting out. He thought about the work his father had done as chairman of the parish council for 25 years, and he thought of the bench that was placed in the park with his father's name on it. He thought of the honour given to his father in the village hall where the memorial service was held, and a plaque naming him as the person who opened the hall, even though he'd been too ill in his final days to actually be there for the opening ceremony.

Thomas met up with one of his dad's sisters, someone he hadn't seen for many years, as it's not usual in the religion that he'd been a part of to mix with relatives who are not members of that religion. He told her that he'd left the religion, and as he expected, she said how happy his father would be to hear that. Thomas felt close to his father at that moment.

He thought of all the wisdom he might have

gained from his father if only he had known how to speak to him. He tried to think back to the earliest moment in his childhood when he might have started to know his father. Then he wondered how much of his father was in *him*, and felt a sudden flurry of happiness as he thought of them both laughing hysterically to Ken Dodd and his Diddy Men.

3 REPENT AT LEISURE

I got married 3 months before my 16th birthday. I was sure it was what I wanted to do. She was much older than me, but everyone told me how much she loved me. I believed it too. We'd never spoken directly about it, well not in person, but like I said, lots of my friends knew her and said that it would be the best decision I would ever make. As I was only 15, my mother gave consent. She did it willingly, and was very happy about it. I knew my father would never approve, so we didn't even tell him at the time.

I'd heard it said before that day that men often marry their mothers, and I wasn't completely repulsed by that idea. I mean, of course I would never want to literally marry my mother, but I loved my mother more than anyone else in the world, and from what I'd heard, this woman did seem to have many of my mother's traits. I wish now that I'd really got to know her properly.

When it came to saying the vows, I got into a complete muddle. I got through them ok, but I was panicking on the inside, as I really didn't understand some of what I was agreeing to.

Things went well for quite a long time. I didn't know what to expect though, so I didn't really know how I was supposed to feel. There were a few things that were challenging. The first thing was that she monitored almost everything I did, and she had very strict rules. I was still finishing school when we first got married, and school was particularly difficult. I was only allowed to be friends with people who knew my wife and whom she considered to be her friends. I could be civil to other people, but if I got into deep conversations, the only thing I was supposed to talk about was my wife and how great she is. I didn't find that difficult to do, as I had been hearing how wonderful she is since I was about 8 years old; that was when my mum first met her. Looking back on that aspect of it, the weirdest part was that she made me write down all the hours that I spent talking about her. If I didn't spend a certain number of hours doing so, she would get quite concerned. It was almost as if she didn't trust my loyalty. Sometimes, I just enjoyed chatting about other things, and I did actually play cards with some people at school, who were not her friends, but I didn't really say much about that. Thankfully, I had at some point said something to most of them about my wife, and I think that's why I didn't feel too bad about it. What would really upset her was not letting someone know I was married to her. It was years before I dared to make friends and not mention it, but a lot happened before I got to that point.

The next big thing was finishing school. I did pretty well at school and I think I could have gone on further, but she was completely against higher education. I guess I quite liked being different in some ways, and I didn't really mind finishing school at 16. Her main priority was my devotion to her, and even though she liked me to provide financially, the main thing was the hours I spent praising her to others. I became very good at finding part-time jobs that could just about enable us to get by.

My entire social network after I left school was made up of people who were completely devoted to my wife. At school I'd taken a bit of abuse about being married to her, but I'd been told to expect that from people who didn't know her. I was even told to feel sorry for them. Yes, I suppose that was it, I actually felt pity for most people.

My father had no time for her, but he was never a real communicator so I didn't have any reason to think there was any substance to his animosity. And it really was animosity; on one occasion he threw my mum's clothes out of the window because she was encouraging us children to get to know the woman who would later become my wife. Obviously, that was before I got married, and as I'd only heard so many good things about her, I found my father's behaviour really shocking. My father even got hold of a book that was purportedly written by someone who'd known my future wife years earlier. Of course, my mum wouldn't read it, and when my dad read a few bits out loud, my mum just said none of it was true. I never did get to hear what the book said, but my mother told me it was simply a load of malicious lies.

My wife absolutely forbade any contact with anyone who'd stopped being friends with her. That wasn't a problem for years, as no one I knew had ever stopped being friends with her, but I did know that if it were to happen, I would have to stop speaking to that person permanently.

My life was fine, but as I say, I didn't know what else a life could be like. Then one day, I heard from my brother that a really close friend of ours had started saying he had some serious concerns about my wife. At that stage, the horror of this news was so incredible that we just knew he was either very unwell, or had somehow been deceived. The biggest concern in such circumstances is that the person has actually read a slanderous book about my wife. Even though we all knew such books were full of lies, we'd also been told ever since childhood that they are powerful, as are the people who write them, and that anyone reading them would almost certainly be lost. My brother and I went to see our friend. We were nervous, but our deep sense of pity for him, as well as our absolute loyalty to my wife, meant that we had to go and try to help him, and if nothing else, know that we'd done all we could to defend my wife's name.

Initially it felt as if there was no hope. It turned out that his sister, who knew of my wife, but was not considered a friend, had given him one of the books described above. He wouldn't have dared show it to us, and we could tell he was deeply embarrassed to admit he'd even looked at such a thing, but he assured us that the concerns he had about my wife were not based on the book, but on things he'd worked out himself. We could hardly treat any of his words seriously after we knew he'd been reading one of those books. We did all we could to remind him of the wonderful qualities of my wife, and by the end of the visit he was pretty convinced. He said that we'd snatched him out of the fire. We came away feeling quite relieved.

A few weeks later, we followed up with another visit. I don't think he ever admitted that he'd read the book again, but he was bringing up several things that called my wife's honesty into question, and there was no other conclusion to be drawn. He did mention a couple of things that gave me pause for thought, but we were so on guard against anything that he might say, that we dismissed everything as nonsense. I even remember saying that if one particular thing he'd said about my wife were true, it still wouldn't make any difference to me. It was something about my wife's ability to accurately predict the future. All of us absolutely trusted my wife on that score, and yet he was calling into question the truthfulness of the fundamental teaching she'd revealed years before, that proved the days we are living in are the end times. We all based our lives on the urgency of the times because of that prophecy. I said that even if she had got that wrong, I would still trust her. He was visibly shocked by my words, but my devotion at that time was complete. We left his house with the feeling that it was only a matter of time before my wife would cut him off. We both knew what that meant, and he did too. He said something to us as we were leaving that stuck with me for many years:

"I will never stop loving all of you, but it will be you that stops loving me."

Sure enough, a few weeks later it was reported that he had apparently negatively influenced his mother and his on/off girlfriend at the time, about my wife, and so he we were all told that my wife was no longer friends with him and that we must never speak to him again. About a month later, his girlfriend was cut off as well because she continued to be friends with him. No longer being a friend of my wife because they had spoken against her was the worst way of losing her friendship. Just breaking one of her rules is bad enough, but to influence others against her is the worst of all crimes. Not only would we never speak to them again, but we were also to think of them as dangerous. Rumours of their further slander about my wife swirled around. Most were unsubstantiated, but it was easy for most people to believe them, especially if the story was connected with a mention of them reading one of the forbidden books; for individuals who read those books, any amount of evil is possible to believe.

I didn't see or speak to either of them again for the next 10 years, and apart from the nagging feeling I had about his final words to me, I was happy to obey my wife's rules.

The next thing that happened quite literally turned my world upside down. A few years later, one more of my closest friends was cut off by my wife. This time it was nothing to do with speaking against her, but simply a small misdemeanour that he'd committed. He desperately sought help for his weakness and he wanted to remain friends with my wife. It deeply troubled me.

My wife did have a mechanism in place for those who are cut off, in order to regain her friendship, and that had always seemed very fair on her part, but I really couldn't understand why my wife had cut him off when he was clearly so sorry about what he'd done. The cutting off is supposed to be just for those who show a brazen attitude. I hadn't known anyone personally who'd succeeded in regaining her friendship, but it had been reported that it was possible in as little as 6 months. My role was simply to not speak to such ones, as was the rule for all of my wife's friends, and the effect would be that after being cut off for a while, they would come to their senses and come begging to my wife, for the friendship to be restored.

You might wonder why I didn't simply ask my wife about the friend, and even ask for an exception to be made. Well, here is where you might start to realise the oddness of our marriage. My wife had such a strong network of friends around her – henchmen, you might say - that it was never really possible to access my wife directly. I had devoted my life to her, but I was only just starting to realise how one directional that love and devotion was.

Three years passed and there was still no sign of my friend coming back to seek my wife's friendship. I was deeply perplexed. I'd felt confused with my other friends mentioned earlier, but because their cutting off involved directly speaking against my wife, I had accepted the idea that they might never return. In fact, there was notion that went around saying that those who are cut off for speaking against my wife, are not permitted to return; the crime is simply too bad.

Anyway, on an impulse, that deep within my heart felt right, I decided to do something I had never done in the entire 29 years of my marriage: I broke the rule about not speaking to someone who'd been cut off by my wife. And it wasn't just a casual meeting up. I met him for dinner. Eating a meal with such a person is absolutely forbidden. I felt tremendous fear of being seen, but I didn't feel that I was doing anything wrong. I had an amazing time with him. I found out that he'd been made to feel so low after being cut off, that he'd actually tried to kill himself. I promised him that day that I would stay in touch with him and support him in any way I could. To my utter surprise, my reaching out to him had the effect of helping him return to seek my wife's forgiveness. I was happy for him, as it meant he could be reunited with so many of his friends and family who'd cut him off for the previous three years.

While he started rebuilding his trust in my wife, I was starting to have serious doubts about her.

On one hand it was so positive that he'd returned, and I felt privileged to have had a part to play in it, but on the other hand, this outcome had come as a direct result of my breaking one of her rules. It made no sense.

There seemed to be a terrifying inevitability concerning the next time I would break the rule. Nothing bad had happened as a result of me seeing this friend, but what would happen if I dared to visit the two who had been cut off for speaking against my wife? As I contemplated it, I remembered those final conversations I'd had with him, and I started thinking that he'd not in my knowledge done anything other than speak about things he was genuinely troubled by.

Yes, he had evidently been poisoned by lies, but did that make him an evil person? I was far too nervous to meet him at that stage, and even when I arranged to meet his girlfriend, yes the same girlfriend, I had no thought that I would follow it up by arranging to meet him. Nevertheless, the meeting with her was lovely and the 10 years vanished instantly. A few weeks later I told her I would be happy to see them both. They invited me for dinner.

I had honestly believed I would never see him again, and here I was voluntarily going into a house to eat food with him. There were knowing smiles on both of our faces as we greeted each other. I was incredibly nervous and had the feeling that I was dancing with the devil. We ate dinner and while we were eating he said he had a video he wanted to show me. Of course I wasn't surprised. So many bad things had been said about him, even stories that he himself had actually given some of those books to people, that it should have come as no shock to me that he now had videos to help spread more negativity about my wife. 'Oh well,' I thought, 'I wanted to see him and I must have had reasons for doing so, so I might as well experience everything.' In some ways, I felt damned just by being there, so why stop at that? The video started playing.

I'm not really sure what I thought would appear, but I expected something unpleasant, or at least many troubling points about my wife that I would have to try to defend. What came up on the screen could not have been more startlingly different. It was the story of our lives... memories from the previous 30 years. Of course, nothing from the missing 10 years appeared, but a seemingly endless stream of happy moments from childhood onwards. It was endless, as we never got to the end of the video by the time I had to leave. For the first half an hour I was just waiting for the screen to go fuzzy and then a different type of programme to start playing, but after a couple of hours, I just settled into the knowledge that this evil person was simply wanting to share reminiscences of our shared lives.

He didn't need to *say* anything.

It took me a few months more to realise it, but finally I understood in what way it's dangerous to see people like that. The thing you will find out if you see people that have stopped being friends with my wife is that they are just the same people they were before. They might even have grown as people and developed even lovelier qualities than they had before, as I have witnessed since becoming reacquainted with these two very special friends. It's not what they might show you that's dangerous, it is simply the fact that they have moved on with their lives. And any negativity they might mention is simply about how being cut off has affected them, which is similar to the content of many of those forbidden books.

That happy reunion opened the door to every

other question that I should have already asked. If the danger around ex-friends was untrue, what else had I been told that might not be true? I thought about the sum total of things that this friend had done which constituted him a person that must never ever be spoken to, and I came up with a list of 4 things:

- He had some concerns about some of the predictions my wife had made, and had done some serious historical research, which uncovered some lies and cover-ups.
- One person who my wife had also cut off had asked to borrow a book from him and he'd lent it to her.
- He had spoken to his own mother and his girlfriend about his concerns.
- A customer of his, who happened to be my mother's neighbour, had asked him about his life story and he told her what had happened regarding being cut off by my wife, and by extension his entire community. This neighbour subsequently refused to engage in conversations with my mother about my wife, as she felt that what had been done was very wrong.

So after more than 30 years of marriage, which I now realise was a sham of a marriage, I have stopped speaking about my wife to people. I no longer report to her about the time I spend talking about her, and I now enjoy friendships with many people who've never even heard of my wife. Sadly, my mother and three of my siblings continue to be devoted to her. I cannot tell them my feelings because I will be viewed as dangerous and they will never speak to me again. But for myself, I now know that what I trusted in for so long contains many lies. And that to stop me ever working out the truth, I was steered away from education, I was taught that critical thinking is arrogance, I was shielded from any meaningful conversations with those who'd been through a similar thing and come out the other side, and I spent many hours every single day reading or telling people about material my wife had prepared that confirmed what a loving person she is.

The incredible part is that I voluntarily did all of it. I myself devoted the best years of my life to spreading a message that is based on half-truths, misquotes and outright lies.

It is a shocking thing that while the abusive relationship is over, and I am free, my family members continue to devote themselves to my wife, and while they still speak to me, it is very much on the condition that I never say anything bad about the person who controlled and manipulated me for decades.

Now I totally understand why my friend happened to tell my mum's neighbour what he'd been through. After suffering with years of post traumatic stress because of being cut off from the only community of people he'd ever known, being lied about, his character maligned in so many ways, and being described as a mentally diseased apostate, one day he just happened to tell someone his experience because she showed him a morsel of human kindness.

4 THE GOLDEN RULE

"You're not going to believe it; I think this is one of them coming to the door right now. I guess you might know her. Do you want me to chat to her? I can try to raise some of the things you're feeling."

"Wow! What a coincidence. Yes, it would be interesting."

"Great. Sit out there by the telephone table. I'm not sure I believe in coincidences." She smiled and headed out towards the front door.

"Ok. Thank you, Judy"

Judy went to the door, and as she opened it, she gave a look of confusion and mild annoyance.

"Yes? Can I help you?"

"Good morning. I'm calling on all your

neighbours this morning and asking a question: Do you think there is anywhere we can go for satisfying answers to all of our difficult questions?"

Judy shut her eyes momentarily and jerked her head back in a way that suggested she'd been bowled over by the oddness of such a question. Then she shook her head gently as she spoke. "I'm sorry. I've got no idea what you're talking about. Of course, I understand the question, but it's just so random. Are you doing a survey?"

The lady standing on the doorstep smiled. It was the sort of smile that one puts on when trying to show incredible patience to a 5-year-old child. "No, we're not doing a survey. I'm actually hoping to share some wonderful good news with you from the Bible. May I ask, do you have a belief in God?"

"Wow! These questions get deeper and deeper. May I ask you a question that might be a bit more basic?"

The smile got even bigger. "Of course. I would be delighted to answer any of your questions."

"Would you like a cup of tea?"

"Oh, that's so kind of you." She looked at her watch. "Well, that would be lovely, thank you. I am with a few friends in your neighbourhood today. Would you mind if I just texted one of them to say that someone has kindly invited me in?"

"Not at all. I'll put the kettle on. Come through."

She stepped through the door, and carefully unzipped her boots and placed them by the front door."

Judy turned around to see if she was following her through to the kitchen. "There's no need to take your boots off. I have a dog, so the floor is not that clean. You might be safer to keep them on." She smiled.

"Oh no, it's fine. We always take our shoes off."

"Ok, well, there's really no need. Anyway, come on through."

She closed the door behind her and walked though to the kitchen, busily tapping a message on her phone while she did so. She then put the phone into her bag and stood in the middle of the large kitchen. "Oh, what a lovely house you have. Have you lived here a long time?"

Judy was filling the kettle. "You certainly like asking questions."

"Oh, I'm sorry. I didn't mean to be rude. I was just meaning that you've decorated the house so beautifully."

"No it's fine. I'm just interested in what you're doing." She smiled at her and pointed to the stools by the breakfast bar. "Take a seat there. You can chat to me while I make the tea."

"Thank you so much. And thank you so much for inviting me in. It was getting a bit chilly out there."

"So, first of all, can I ask whether I am speaking to a Jehovah's Witness, or perhaps a Mormon, or are you from another group?"

She beamed now. "No, you got it right first time. I am one of Jehovah's Witnesses."

"Isn't it unusual for you to be on your own? Normally your people come to my door in twos, and sometimes with a couple of children too."

She gave a little laugh. "Yes, we are often in twos. Today we were an odd number so I said I would do a few doors on my own."

"I see. And have you had a good morning?"

"Yes, lovely. Not many people in, but it's really good to be out."

Judy opened a cupboard and took out a couple of teabags and popped them into two mugs that she took from the draining board. "I must say, I've often wondered why you call on weekday mornings. Don't you think it would be better to call when people are actually at home? I mean most people go out to work in this close. "

"Yes, we try to call at all sorts of times. We often call at weekends too."

"I see. So, going back to your original question. You asked about finding satisfying answers. I presume you are referring to the Bible as a place to find them. Is that right?"

"Yes, we have found that the Bible can give us guidance in so many different areas of life. Have you ever studied the Bible?"

Judy poured boiling water into the mugs. "I studied it a bit when I was at university, but it was more as a piece of literature."

"I see. Well could I show you something that has really helped me in my life?"

"Certainly." Judy took some milk from the fridge. "Do you take milk and sugar?"

"Just a little milk, please. By the way, my name is Karen, may I ask your name?"

"Yes, I'm Judy."

"Oh, what a lovely name."

"Really! Even though it's usually linked to Punch and Judy?"

"Oh yes, I never thought of that." She laughed

again.

Judy put two mugs of tea on the counter, and sat on a stool facing Karen. "There we are."

"Thank you so much. A lovely cup of tea." Karen had been busy tapping away on her tablet. "Now, here is the verse I wanted to show you." She held the tablet towards Judy and pointed to the words as she read aloud: "Do to others as you would have them do to you."

"Oh yes, I am familiar with those words."

"And don't you think the world would be a better place if everyone lived by them?'

"Yes, I daresay it would. Can I ask you another question?"

"Of course. Go ahead." She smiled excitedly.

"Now, I may have got this wrong, but Jehovah's Witnesses claim to live by the Bible, is that right?"

"Yes, we certainly try to."

"Ok, so let's just take that bit you read to me, and let me ask you about how you would have others do things to you, so that we can work out how you will treat them. Is that ok?"

"Yes, of course. I would like to be treated with

kindness."

"Ok, but let's think of a particular situation. Just say you were in my position. I'm a Catholic. In name only really as I don't go to Church very much, but let's just say I decided to stop being a Catholic and decided to join your religion. Now remember, you are imagining yourself as me. So, if you were in that situation, and you told your family you were going to stop being a Catholic and wanted to join the Jehovah's Witnesses, how would you like them to treat you?"

"That's funny you should say that, because my family didn't react well when I became a Witness." She smiled.

"Interesting. But, but how would you have *liked* them to treat you?"

"Well, with respect. We all have freedom of choice."

"Good. I agree. And when you say with respect, would you like them to treat you as they did before you made that decision?"

"Yes, certainly. I wish they had actually. In the end they have accepted it, but they don't agree with everything I do."

"Ok, now let's take it a tiny bit further. How would you like the friends you had before you became a

Witness to treat you after you have made the switch?"

"The same. With respect and kindness."

"That's great. So, let's bring in those words you read to me. So, if that is how you would like people to do things to you, how would you treat someone who decided to stop being a Jehovah's Witness?"

At this point, Karen closed the cover on her tablet, and took a swig of tea. "Well, I would *try* to treat them with respect."

"Right. So if they told you they were no longer going to be a Witness and that they wanted to explore other religious ideas, you'd be fine with that?"

Karen took a gulp of tea. "This is lovely tea."

"Thank you. Yes, I always use Yorkshire Tea. So, going back to the question. According to that passage from the Bible, how would you treat someone who no longer wanted to be a Witness?"

"That is a very good question. I might have to go home and do a bit of research on that."

"Really? But I thought you said that if we lived by those words you read, the world would be a better place."

"Yes, it really would, but some situations are complicated."

"Ok. I only ask because I've heard that Jehovah's Witnesses have been known to totally stop talking to certain ones if they stop being a Witness. Is that not true?"

She drained the last bit of tea from the mug. "Well, that would only be in certain circumstances."

"I see. What about a son or daughter? I've even heard that some Witness parents will not speak to their own child if they leave the religion. Do you have any children?"

"Yes, I have a son and daughter."

"And are they in the religion?"

"No, I'm afraid not. My son was never interested, but very sadly my daughter did come along until she was in her 20s and then she stopped."

"And do you see your son or daughter?"

"Well, I see my son. He works for my husband. He pops in most days. But no, I haven't seen my daughter for a while."

"That must be very sad."

"Yes, it broke my heart actually."

"I'm so sorry to hear that. And what about the paradise that Witnesses often talk about? Do you believe in that?"

"Oh yes. We believe we are very close to the time when Jehovah God will bring an end to all the suffering and will bring about a paradise."

"And if your son and daughter don't join you in the religion before it comes, will they be in paradise?"

"We believe that Jehovah will read hearts, so I really hope he will give them a chance."

"What if he doesn't? Will you enjoy being in paradise without your children?"

At this point, Karen started to cry. "I'm so sorry. I don't know why I'm crying."

"Don't worry at all, it's quite normal to cry. I cry all the time." She reached out and touched Karen's hand.

"Anyway, thank you so much for the tea. I really must let you get on. I am so sorry about crying. I am a bit sad about my daughter."

"If you don't mind me saying so, it sounds a bit like you're not being allowed to treat your daughter as you would like to treat her."

"Oh no, it's not like that. We all make our own decisions."

"I see. So if your daughter walked in now and said she loved you and wanted to have a relationship with you, what would you say?"

"Well, I do love her very much, but I have to be obedient to Jehovah's discipline."

"Oh, that's a new piece of the puzzle. You hadn't mentioned that before. So if someone wants to stop being a Witness, they have to be disciplined?"

"No, not exactly? Anyway, I really must be going now." She stood up from the stool and slipped the tablet into her handbag.

"I really don't mean to upset you, but I would like to understand how this discipline situation works."

"I'll do some research and maybe I could see you another time."

"That would be great. But just so you know exactly what I want to know, can I explain about a situation I heard about? Just quickly, and then I'll let you go."

Karen looked at her watch. "Ok, just quickly then. My friends will wonder where I've got to."

"No problem. I'll just outline the situation. I heard of a girl who had been sexually abused by one of the elders in the Jehovah's Witness religion. She told her mother and father, and the father told another one of the elders. Well, to cut a very long story short, the elders met with the girl, and asked her all the details. They then confronted the elder. He denied it, and that was the end of the matter. Nothing was reported to the police and the elder continued being an elder. Later, he moved away, and finally, several years later, two more girls came forward and brought a case against him. They were no longer Witnesses and they went to the police and he ended up going to prison. The original girl suffered terribly for many years because of the abuse she'd experienced. When she found out what had finally happened to her abuser, she felt even more let down by the elders and felt that them not believing her had led to more girls being abused. Finally, she decided to stop being a Witness, and once she made her decision known to the congregation, everyone, including her own parents, stopped speaking to her. So my question is this: Does Jehovah want a girl who has been abused and who has been let down by her community, to be disciplined further by having her family and friends cut her off because she no longer wants to be in that religion?"

Karen broke down in tears. Judy left her stool and went and hugged her. "I'm so sorry. I don't mean to cry. We so need the paradise. That's all I'm looking forward to." She was sobbing into Judy's arms.

"Karen, I don't know what you're really thinking deep in your heart, but I think you need to start treating your daughter as *you* would like to be treated."

"I know." She was struggling to speak. "I just must be obedient."

"You've said that a few times, Karen, but it seems to me that that verse you read earlier would be the best thing to be obedient to."

There was a cough from across the room. Karen jumped slightly and looked to where the sound came from.

"Hello, Mum."

5 SAMOSAS

"It's been going on for years. Everyone who gets things from her ends up having problems."

"What are you saying? How do they have problems?"

"Demons."

"Are you serious? "

"Yes, totally. Especially second-hand things."

"But what are the problems? How could you possibly be sure they're connected to the things she gives people?"

"It's happened too many times. Everyone in a family is happy and doing fine, and then one of them gets given 'the uniform' when they start getting involved with *her*, and that's when the problems begin."

"The uniform?"

"Oh, you must have seen it. They look perfectly normal, wearing ordinary clothes, and then gradually the image changes. And it's always some kind of vintage outfit. Those stupid tweedy suits."

"But isn't that just a fashion that they're drawn to?"

"No, there have just been too many problems to ignore it?"

Tom was resolute in not buying into this nonsense, but he was careful not to wear the uniform, or be given clothing by her that would identify him as one of her 'clan'. He was actually attracted to the style, but he resented the idea that if he wore any of it, he would be seen as a drone of this woman and somehow under her spell (pun intended). He didn't for one minute believe any of the stories about items of clothing containing demons. To him, it was just finding a scapegoat to carry the blame for whatever problems were going on.

These whisperings were often taking place in the congregation about this poor woman, Felicity. It's a very strong religious community in which most of those who've grown up in it believe that Satan is to blame for everything that goes wrong, and that his wishes can be carried out by his workers, the demons. And in some mysterious way, demons can be found in certain articles that have had some connection with spiritism, and the dark arts. It is not difficult to see how a virtual witch-hunt could develop around a person in such a community who does things a little differently and who has an interest in antique fashions, and giving away lots of second-hand items that would have come from the houses of people who are not in their religion, and who might very likely have been dabbling in stuff that was connected with the occult, which equated in their beliefs to Satan.

Nevertheless, one day when he popped in with a friend and had a cup of tea and a chat with Felicity, he was happy to accept the bag of samosas she gave him. He was a little paranoid about taking items of clothing, but surely none of her critics would suggest demons would enter the samosas.

Tom was lodging in the house of a very nice older couple, and they were not connected to his religion. He just rented a room upstairs, but could use the kitchen facilities to cook meals. He rarely did cook, but he did make use of a shelf assigned to him in the fridge, and mainly kept things for breakfast in there. That particular day he saw Wendy, the wife, when he went to the fridge to store his samosas.

"Hello, Wendy. How are you?"

"Not bad, Tom, thank you."

"I have a big bag of samosas that a friend gave

me. There are more here than I can eat, so if you or Bill want one, please help yourselves."

"Thanks, Tom. Actually Bill does love samosas."

"Well I've not tried them yet, but my friend orders them from the place that she says makes the best samosas in the city."

He placed them on his shelf in the fridge and went upstairs to his room.

He was often out all day, and sometimes could go a whole day, and maybe even two, without seeing Wendy or Bill. The next day, he went out to work before either of them were up and he came home very late that night after being at a friend's house. The day after that he again left in the morning without seeing them, but they were both in the living room when he came back about 4 o'clock on that second day. He would often just slip past the room and go upstairs, but sometimes there would be a brief exchange. It seemed like this would be one of those days. As he passed the door, Wendy called out.

"Hello Tom. Could you pop in here for a minute?"

He pushed the door open, and although the way she'd called him in was unusual, and he was slightly alarmed, he tried to sound as friendly as ever. "Of course. Hello Bill. Hi Wendy."

Wendy was the one who spoke, but Bill looked pretty serious. "Tom, we are very upset about something."

Tom knew he'd gone red, but he had no idea what he might have done. "Oh dear, I'm so sorry to hear that."

"We really don't know why you would do such a thing, and we've never had any problems with you before, but when you went out this morning, you left *all* the taps on in the bathroom – the sink and the bath taps!"

"I don't know what to say," and he really didn't, "I would never do such a thing, but I honestly don't know how to explain it."

Bill spoke next. "The thing is Tom, it would be bad enough if you'd just done it the once, but you did exactly the same thing yesterday morning."

"As I said, I really don't know what to say. If I did do it, I cannot even imagine how I could have done it without realising. I am so sorry."

Wendy responded: "Well, like I said, we've had no problems with you before, but this really is quite serious. It feels very disrespectful."

A few minutes later, Tom was in his room, relieved that they weren't chucking him out straight away, but completely confused by the whole story. Then a thought entered his mind that he refused to let in... 'Could it be the samosas?' There was no way he was going to tell Bill and Wendy that maybe a demon had entered their plumbing via the samosas. It was stupid.

He soon had to go out again and he wasn't going to be back until late. He was glad that he wouldn't have to face them again until the next day. He decided to leave the samosas in the fridge until later.

It was after 11 when he came back through the garden gate and headed to the back door. He was feeling oddly nervous about going back in. As he walked up the path with the house in darkness, he saw through the glass pane of the front door the shape of a young child running up the stairs. He was terrified. He let himself in and turned on almost all of the lights. He went up to his room and dumped all of his stuff. He tried to decide what to do. If he hadn't left the lights on downstairs, he would've been too scared to go back down again. He picked up his house keys and headed to the kitchen. He opened the fridge, saw the bag of samosas that had not been touched since he placed it there two days before, grabbed it and went out the back door, locking it behind him. He initially thought of dumping them in the dustbin at the side of the house, but instead he went out the gate and made for the row of shops on the main road. He threw the bag of samosas in a bin by the newsagents. He was sad he never even got to try one.

Bill and Wendy were a bit weird with him for the rest of that week, but there were no more occurrences of him leaving all the taps on, and neither did he see the little girl running up the stairs again.

6 I'M SO SORRY

She was good at putting him at ease, not because the environment was relaxing, but for exactly the opposite reason. The first time he saw her it was in her own home, and having not long ago seen The Matrix, the meeting bore an uncanny resemblance to Neo's meeting with the Oracle. There were no people in a waiting room bending spoons, but there were far too many family members wandering around to make it seem like a discreet counselling session. She wasn't making cookies, but she was insistent on finishing a few chores before leading him into a downstairs spare bedroom that doubled as an office. The whole thing put him at ease simply because it felt chaotic and ordinary.

He really couldn't quite believe he was there, but he knew he had to do something, even if it was just to reassure his boss that he was seeking help after the uncontrollable crying she'd witnessed in her office three weeks earlier. All she'd done was question his judgment over a paragraph he'd put forward for inclusion in the company's annual report. Admittedly he had felt out of his depth in writing it, but he really wanted to say something meaningful and he felt strongly that a more determined effort to market children's books would make economic sense. She used an expression that almost meant nothing to him at the time, but would grow in significance as the years passed:

"This is purely based on anecdotal evidence", she said.

The counsellor had been recommended to him and everything about her so far made him see why. It was truly mad. He had no idea what a counsellor should be like. The 'Empath', Deanna Troi, from Star Trek Next Generation came to his mind, but he doubted the woman in front of him was half Betazoid. She was a member of the same religion as him and this had made it seem somehow acceptable. Within their particular religion, speaking to anyone other than the elders about personal problems would be frowned upon. He was an elder himself, and he certainly couldn't imagine telling his fellow elders about breaking down in floods of tears at work, and for no apparent reason. He'd actually cried for half an hour, and it was real sobbing. It was a brilliant way to deflect from the mild telling-off the boss had given him, but she was clearly mortified by what she'd reduced him to. She went and made him tea and was incredibly consoling. She reassured him with another meaningful expression:

"You are in a completely safe place here. We are not part of your religious world, but we can be supportive."

He thanked her so much for her understanding and said he would seek some help with whatever was playing on his mind.

He remembered talking a lot about the crying in his boss's office, and about his dad's death, which he thought might be relevant. He talked about the pressure he felt under to be available to so many people. The first thing she observed about him was how often he said sorry. This comment made him laugh, but not uncontrollably at first. Then she asked him why he said sorry so often and whether he felt he *should* feel sorry on each occasion. This made him laugh more. He then related to her a story of a particularly demanding situation. As an elder, he had responsibility to support a certain number of individuals within the congregation. One man, who had previously been an elder but had stopped because of mental health issues, was seriously struggling to cope with life. But it was his wife who proved to be the most demanding. One night, he'd arrived home late and he found 10 messages from her on his answering machine, each message becoming more and more frantic. As it turned out, there wasn't a particular problem, but it was just a repeated rant about the fact that they needed more support. The counsellor asked him what he did to support them and he listed quite a few things. Then she asked him what he said to this couple the next time he saw them. He thought for a few seconds and was already laughing by the time he told her the word: "Sorry." Or more specifically, "I'm so sorry!" She laughed too. He laughed so much for the next half an hour that it made the crying in his boss's office look quite mild. He rolled on the floor for some of it. The counsellor was also laughing and seemed to be urging him on. If laughter therapy was what she intended, then she was good at her job, and the session was so memorable that he really did take charge of his future apologies. The few comments she made between laughs were helpful. She told him that apologising when you don't need to feel guilty is tantamount to inviting a person to abuse your kindness or to take advantage.

In the following months, he was astonished to find out that as soon as he stopped apologising to this couple, their demands upon him diminished, and they even became appreciative of what he was able to do for them. He left the session feeling that it really had been worth it, and he saw her twice more after that.

He's prone to nostalgia and by the third visit he was not really saying anything new, but simply reminiscing with her about the laughter session. There didn't seem to be much more happening. He knew that the very thing he was not talking about was the thing that he most needed to talk about, and he also knew that it was exactly because she was in the same religion as him, that he could not talk about it. He assured her that she'd really helped him and thanked her profusely for her time and for the discount she gave to those in the same religion as her.

He didn't really doubt her professionalism and neither did he imagine she wouldn't be able to cope with what he might tell her, but it was his own fear to discuss it that stopped him. In truth, to be a qualified counsellor and a member of their religion was no small thing. Higher education is seriously discouraged, and *going* to a counsellor would be bad enough, so *being* one was even more astonishing. Being a woman in a male dominated religion would have led some to have found her choice of career a brazen disregard of a woman's role, and others to have simply considered her a crazy eccentric. He connected her more closely to the Oracle, as mentioned before, and looking back, he wished he had told her about his homosexual feelings.

If it had achieved nothing more than curtailing his overuse of the word sorry, it had been worthwhile, but it really did achieve more. What he *didn't* tell her, he *thought* about, and that personal admission of what he was really crying about in his boss's office, was perhaps more helpful than anything she might have told him at that time. What could she tell him other than the facts? Within their religion there could be no practicing of homosexuality. According to the discussions he'd had over the years with fellow members of his religion, opinions varied; there were some who thought it would be possible to change one's feelings of attraction from same sex to opposite sex, but the majority didn't believe that homosexual feelings would exist at all unless you *chose* to feel that way.

Sometime after that, he was walking up the high street and he saw a lady riding up the road towards him on a bicycle. It had just started to rain and he was walking fairly briskly to get back to his car. As the woman got closer, he saw that she had a clear plastic bag pulled right down over her face. He felt like putting his hands out to help her, or to scream, but as he stared in wonder, he realised she was smiling beneath the plastic and was in no apparent danger. It might sound like a ridiculous exaggeration to say that his childhood collapsed at that moment, but it really isn't.

His walking slowed right down and he welcomed the rain, as it got heavier. He was completely drenched by the time he got into the car. He even began to wonder if he'd really seen it. For as long as he could remember, any mention of plastic bags was also connected with suffocation. They were always snatched away and put out of reach in the big cupboard in the utility room. If he or any of his siblings took hold of one, even for a few seconds after the shopping was emptied, the following warning would follow: "You must never play with polythene bags, so many children have suffocated from playing with them." The bag would be handed over.

As he sat in the car, lost in the trauma of it, he gradually started to laugh. He thought about whether a person *could* actually suffocate by playing with a plastic bag. And as he thought of the woman on the bike, he suddenly realised that if you found yourself unable to breathe, you would simply pull the bag off. His mind flashed with childish imagery of the bag literally sticking itself to his face and the handles of the bag forcefully grabbing him about the throat and tying themselves in a knot under his chin. He imagined his futile efforts to pull the bag off, and then collapsing helplessly on the kitchen floor. He didn't know whether to blame his mother or his own imagination. Later that night, he rationalised about it and conceded that some danger might exist if his sister had decided to hold the bag over his head, but in their family such a thought seemed extremely out of line with their levels of naughtiness. He wasn't resentful about not being able to play with plastic bags, but the whole episode connected in his mind with the crying in his boss's office, and finally took him to his enormous dictionary. He had a vague idea what it meant, but having left school at 16 and with any thoughts of critical thinking absolutely outlawed, he'd never thought to find out what that expression meant.

Anecdotal evidence: evidence that relies heavily on personal testimonies.

This was the first time that he experienced

something similar to what was described concerning the Apostle Paul – scales fell from his eyes. His mistake at work was not a deliberate manipulation of information, but it was simply proving a point in the only way he had ever been taught to do it. Almost every rule from his childhood onwards was supported by an anecdote, and usually an anecdote of uncertain origin. Did his mother really know of so many children who had suffocated from playing with plastic bags? This was only the beginning.

He thought through the many rules and restrictions imposed by his religion, and nearly all of them were supported by one or two anecdotes of someone who had broken a rule and the dire consequences that followed, or of someone who obeyed it and the countless blessings they reaped as a result. Even the rules that were supported by verses from the Bible were strongly dependent on a prescribed interpretation. But by far the majority of the rules were enforced and supported solely by anecdote. His dictionary wandering led him to 'empirical evidence', and that is when he felt alarmed and cheated. How many of the rules he'd lived by had any substance to them other than someone else's experience, or worse still, opinion?

At the age of 15, when he got baptized, it was he himself who metaphorically put the plastic bag over his head and voluntarily allowed the strangulation. And as he thought back through the painful battles he'd fought in order to obey the rules, and the relationships and love he'd been denied, it was he that always said, 'I'm so sorry, it's my fault.'

So strong was the hold, that it was many years before he escaped the religion that was suffocating his own conscience, as well as his personal quest for spirituality, whatever that might turn out to mean.

7 SPECIAL STUDY ARTICLE 1

A FAITHFUL AND DISCREET SLAVE[4] WHO STOPS BEATING HIS FELLOW SLAVES

'My Yoke is easy and my burden is light' – Matthew 11:30

1. To provide the scriptural basis for these changes, we want to direct your attention to the theme text, Matthew 11:28 – 30: "Come to me, all you who are weary and burdened, and I will give you rest. Take my yoke upon you and learn from me, for I am gentle and humble in heart, and you will find rest for your souls. For my yoke is easy and my burden is light." After meditating very deeply upon these verses, it is clear that we need to learn from Jesus even more fully.

---

[4] The Governing Body of Jehovah's Witnesses, which at the time of publication comprises 8 men, is thought by Jehovah's Witnesses to be the Faithful and Discreet Slave referred to in Matthew Chapter 24.

2. Jesus is gentle and humble in his heart and promises to bring refreshment to all of his followers. Over the past year, the assembly programmes have focused on the idea of not giving up. It has become very obvious that many have become tired and in some cases, are close to giving out completely. This has indicated that the messages being conveyed by means of certain teachings have not been providing refreshment. This will now change.

3. In Matthew chapter 24, where we find the verses about a faithful and discreet slave, we also find a very stark warning about that faithful and discreet slave becoming an evil slave who starts to beat his fellow slaves (Matthew 24:45-51). While we hope that the faithful and discreet slave has not started to beat his fellow slaves, the words of our Master, Jesus, provide a strong warning never to risk burdening his faithful followers with teachings that are far from refreshing.

4. Before discussing some of the changes that are being addressed in this article, it would be good for us to give consideration to the illustration of a faithful and discreet slave being used to manage the affairs of a household. Where there is a very large house and a large household, there would often be a body of servants that would relieve the master of the house of many of the mundane duties involved in caring for all the members of that household. The master would be delighted in having a body of servants who can be depended upon to carry out their tasks in exactly the

way they know the master likes things to be done, hence the word 'faithful'.

5. The word 'discreet' is also interesting. Discreet is defined as being very careful in word and action in order to keep something secret, or to avoid causing embarrassment to someone. In the context of this illustration, we might think of servants quietly and discreetly going about their tasks, not drawing undue attention to themselves, and not causing the master embarrassment by acting in any way that would reflect badly upon his reputation.

6. Linking Jesus' words from our theme text about him being gentle and humble, with the illustration of a faithful and discreet slave dutifully, yet discreetly, carrying out the wishes of his master, we see that a shift in behaviour is vital. While those hoping to be viewed by Jesus as the faithful and discreet slave have done what they thought was right in the way they've been managing things, it is time to learn more carefully from the Master, Christ, and to carry out future activities in a way that truly reflects the personality and qualities of Christ.

7. It would be an embarrassment to the master of a house if one of his servants interrupted a meal that the master was hosting, stood on a table and started barking his own commands at all the other members of the household. Of course, the servant might say that he is simply reinforcing things he knows the master likes,

but if his manner of speaking is contrary to the personality of the master, then the master would not be at all pleased with such an outburst. Also, if the servant is truly discreet and he genuinely feels that there is a problem that needs to be addressed, he would quietly speak to the master and await his instruction on the matter.

8. For some time now we have provided a monthly television broadcast, thus making good use of modern technology to reach Jesus' followers in their own homes. Many have derived encouragement from these programmes, but there have been reports from some other faithful ones that indicate that some talks and videos have gone far 'beyond what is written,' (1 Corinthians 4:6), and have thus been a source of anxiety, and in some cases, discouragement. While the use of technology is not necessarily inappropriate, it is vital that what is presented truly reflects the personality of Jesus, and that the words of a servant never become more significant than the words of the master.

9. With the forgoing in mind, we can now announce some changes that might seem somewhat surprising. With the idea of surprise in mind, think of the word surprise in the context of an exciting gift, and not a terrible shock. Jesus' way of dealing with people while he was on earth was constantly surprising. The way he reacted to the woman recently healed of a flow of blood, and the way he told a chief tax collector to hurry down from a tree because he was going to stay in

his house, were definitely surprising moments for the onlookers, (Luke 8:42b – 48; 19:1-7). Lowly ones were used to being treated harshly, or at least distantly and officiously. Jesus, true to his words from our theme text, was gentle and humble.

10. The first matter we are going to address is how we are to view those who as yet don't appear to be following Jesus in the way that we understand to be the correct way. It has been a habit to use the term 'worldly' and to think of such ones as a bad influence and not ones to be associated with beyond necessary contact in school or in the workplace. The term 'worldly' is not found in scripture and if we try to find the concept of it in the Bible, the closest we come to it would be the very term the Pharisees used to describe the common people. The word 'amharets,' meaning 'people of the land,' was used by the Pharisees as a term of contempt, to mean that they were accursed, principally because they were uneducated and ignorant of all the rabbinic laws (John 7:49). When we compare this to Jesus' treatment of the common people, including sinners, we start to see why a drastic change in our thinking is necessary.

11. As mentioned before, Jesus hurried to the house of a chief tax collector that he might stay the night there and benefit from the hospitality that the tax collector would extend to him. Rather than condemning the man, as most people would have done, Jesus made the man feel special and worthy of attention. The result

of this treatment can be read in Luke 19:8-10: 'Zacchaeus stood up and said to the Lord: "Look, Lord! Here and now I give half of my possessions to the poor, and if I have cheated anybody out of anything, I will pay back four times the amount." At this, Jesus said to him: "Today salvation has come to this house, because this man, too, is a son of Abraham. For the Son of man came to seek and to save the lost."'

12. Jesus didn't affect this great change in the man by condemning him as a gross sinner, and neither did he describe him as a worldly person. Rather, it was by loving him and believing the good in him that Jesus empowered the man to give up his life of badness and evidently become his follower. What can we learn from this? The first step will be to remove the term 'worldly' from our vocabulary and the second step will be to make a change in our minds and hearts about how we view all the people we come into contact with.

13. It is also important at this point to bring an end to the use of the term, 'the truth,' to describe the way we try to live. While we hope we have found some truths and have great confidence in the beliefs that we hold dear, it is arrogant to use a term that indicates that we have the monopoly on truth and think that everyone else is wrong. Based on the fact that we have constantly had to change our teachings, it is clear that we have not yet found the truth in its entirety. In the past we have attributed these changes to the light getting brighter. It is more appropriate to say that we

presumptuously thought we understood something, when in fact we evidently did not. Saying the light has got brighter as a way of explaining a change of teaching is effectively blaming God for failing to give us enough light. We sincerely apologise and seek Jehovah's forgiveness for this previous way of dealing with a change in teaching. From now on, we shall endeavour to ensure that every idea put forward is solidly based on God's own word and where it is not clear from scripture, we will not dogmatically declare what it means.

14. What about those who claim to be Christians, but who have ideas and teachings that run contrary to our understanding of Christ's teachings? Let's consider the occasion when one of the apostles reported to Jesus that a certain man, not following with them, was actually expelling demons by the use of Jesus' name. The apostle John tried to prevent the man because he was not accompanying them. Did Jesus agree with John and condemn the man as a member of false religion and thus as one to be despised? Turn to Mark 9:39-40 to read Jesus' surprising answer: 'Jesus said: "Do not stop him. For no one who does a miracle in my name can in the next moment say anything bad about me, for whoever is not against us is for us."

15. Jesus goes even further in describing how such ones are to be viewed. He goes on to talk about someone who gives his followers a drink of water because they belong to Christ. Surely just giving the

disciples a drink is not sufficient for someone to be viewed as a follower of Jesus. To the contrary, in verse 41 we read Jesus' words about such a person: 'Truly I tell you, anyone who gives a cup of water in my name because you belong to the Messiah, will certainly not lose their reward." Rather than being in judgment of others, as we were prone to previously, we are instead to remember Jesus' command to 'stop judging' and take to heart the next words recorded in Mark chapter 9. Concerning the one who simply gives a drink of water to Jesus' followers because they belong to Christ, Jesus says: "If anyone causes one of these little ones – those who believe in me – to stumble, it would be better for them if a large millstone were hung around their neck and they were thrown into the sea."

16. It is now clear that instead of having an attitude of condemnation and judgment towards those who claim to believe in Christ but who don't want to accompany us in our Christian activity, we should commend them for their faith and rejoice that they are doing what they can for Christ; 'whoever is not against us is for us' (Mark 9:40). If Jesus told his followers to stop judging, then it is evident that the matter of judgment will not rest with humans (Matthew 7:1,2). Our role is to show love and kindness in the way we spread Jesus' teachings to all we meet, and give commendation to those who are making any efforts to exercise faith in him.

17. So then, what is false religion? Who is the

great harlot, Babylon the Great? These questions will be addressed in a future article. For now though, we must continue to give attention to the vital matter of learning from Jesus and being a source of refreshment, just as he was.

18. In paragraph 11 we read Jesus' words recorded at Luke 19:10, that he "came to seek and to save the lost.' It is with these words in mind that we move onto the next matter requiring a drastic change in our thinking. It has been a teaching for many decades that those who are judged as unrepentant for sinful conduct are to be classed as disfellowshipped, and are effectively shunned by all their former brothers and sisters, including their family members. Considering that Jesus came to save what was lost and told his followers to 'stop judging' we will next consider an adjusted understanding of how we are to view wrongdoers. This will be discussed in the next article.

8 SPECIAL STUDY ARTICLE 2

DISFELLOWSHIPPING – A LOVING PROVISION OR AN ACT OF CRUELTY?

"Come to me, all you who are weary and burdened, and I will give you rest." – Matthew 11:28

1. When being accused by the Pharisees of eating with tax collectors and sinners, Jesus said: "It is not the healthy who need a doctor, but the sick. I have not come to call the righteous, but the sinners." (Mark 2:16, 17). Thus, Jesus showed an absolute determination to give attention to those who were despised by the religious leaders of the time, and who in many cases felt wretched and unworthy. It is clear that we must do everything we can to make sure we imitate Jesus and not the Pharisees in how we treat those who commit sins, which as it turns out, is all of us. In fact, by meditating on the sinful condition of us all, we clearly understand why Jesus commanded his

followers to 'stop judging' and to focus on our own shortcomings, rather than notice the errors of others (Matthew 7:1–5).

2. So, how exactly did Jesus deal with sinners? Well, with the aforementioned in mind, it is clear that everyone he dealt with was a sinner, because he was the only human on earth without sin. He was the only human who could rightfully judge others, and yet according to our theme text, he simply promised to bring refreshment to all those who are weary and burdened (Matthew 11:28).

3. Do we see such refreshment being provided in modern times? In some cases, yes, but it is clear that we must give renewed attention to Jesus' perfect example, and remove any arrangements that could be more akin to the behaviour of the Pharisees than anything Jesus stood for. In the time of Jesus, the practice of expelling people was carried out by the Pharisees and one of the capital offenses by which a person could be expelled from the synagogue, was putting faith in Jesus (John 9:22, 12:42). While we have been disfellowshipping people for many decades, it is now vital that we re-examine the Bible verses that have been used to support this practice, and make absolutely sure that we are truly following Jehovah's inspired direction.

4. In this article, we shall address some of the key texts that have been associated with the practice of

disfellowshipping. We shall start with the situation that existed in the congregation in Corinth, which at first glance would seem very much to align itself with the modern day disfellowshipping procedure. Please open your Bibles to 1st Corinthians chapter 5. The first thing to notice is that Paul discusses the matter of an individual's sin with the entire congregation, by means of a letter that was to be read aloud to all. There is no suggestion of elders being used to ascertain the repentance of the man in question. In verse 1 we learn that the sexual immorality existing in this congregation is "of a kind that even pagans do not tolerate: A man sleeping with his father's wife." In verse 2, Paul even asks the members of the congregation if they are proud of it. Evidently, Paul is greatly distressed that instead of upholding God's standards, the congregation is blatantly tolerating a shocking case of immorality. What is to be done?

5. Let's read verses 9 to 11 of 1st Corinthians chapter 5: "I wrote to you in my letter not to associate with sexually immoral people – not at all meaning the people of this world who are immoral, or the greedy and swindlers, or idolaters. In that case you would have to leave the world. But now I am writing to you that you must not associate with anyone who claims to be a brother or sister but is sexually immoral or greedy, an idolater or slanderer, a drunkard or a swindler. Do not eat with such people." Paul adds in verse 13: "Expel the wicked person from among you." Two vital points must

not be ignored in this passage of scripture. First, the man mentioned in verse 1 **is** sleeping with his father's wife. It is not a situation in which he has on one occasion committed immorality with his father's wife; it is a current and an on-going situation. In verse 11, Paul tells the congregation to stop associating with anyone claiming to be a brother or sister who **is** sexually immoral, or, who **is** a greedy person, or, who **is** a drunkard. A person's getting drunk on one occasion does not make him "a drunkard." The words of the apostle Paul clearly relate to a continuing course of life, a characteristic and distinguishing factor of what the person actually **is**. None of this is suggesting that we minimise the seriousness of committing a sin even on just one occasion, but it is important to notice that the strong direction given by Paul in this chapter only relates to those who are continuing in a course of sin.

6. So, to summarise what we have read so far, Paul is disgusted that within the congregation there is a brother who is sleeping with his father's wife and that those in the congregation are condoning it. Paul's clear guidance in this type of situation is to stop associating with such a man. Then what happened? We can be very grateful that Paul's second letter seems to continue with this particular saga. 2nd Corinthians chapter 2, verses 5 to 8 reads as follows: "If anyone has caused grief, he has not so much grieved me as he has grieved all of you to some extent – not to put it too severely. The punishment inflicted on him by the majority is

sufficient. Now instead, you ought to forgive and comfort him, so that he will not be overwhelmed by excessive sorrow. I urge you, therefore, to reaffirm your love for him." Again, it is in a letter to the entire congregation that Paul tells everyone what they should now do with this man. There is no indication of a committee of elders meeting with the man to ascertain his repentance; it is simply a case of forgiving the man for what he had done. It is also noteworthy that Paul says that the punishment given by the majority is sufficient. A majority is not everyone. Paul makes no mention of taking action against a minority who chose not to share in the punishment given to this particular man.

7. Whereas in pre-Christian times, the elders of a city served in a judicial capacity when requested to do so, Christians are not subject to the law system of Israel. As seen by the words of Paul in the chapters we have considered, the ceasing of fellowship with persons pursuing a sinful course was not the result of some formalised judicial procedure. It simply called for voluntary congregational response on a personal level. While, when circumstances required, members were urged to withdraw fellowship for the good of the congregation and its name and with the additional hope that the individual would come to his senses and leave his bad course, there are no instructions telling family members to stop talking to the wrongdoer and neither are there any punitive measures brought against any

who choose not to follow this direction.

8. One last point to notice in 1st Corinthians chapter 5 is that Paul specifically talks about anyone **claiming to be a brother or sister** who is sexually immoral or a greedy person, and so on. What would the situation be when the person is no longer claiming to be a brother or sister, or is no longer thought of as such? Paul is silent on this, but the wording he uses here could indicate that once a person no longer wishes to be thought of as a brother or sister, then there would be no need to take the action Paul describes. There is no shame brought upon a congregation by the actions of a person who has clearly stopped claiming to be a member of it.

9. Next, we will consider Jesus' illustration of the prodigal son. What does this illustration teach us about Jesus' attitude towards those who pursue a life of sin? The illustration is found at Luke chapter 15 verses 11 to 32 (READ). In verse 7 of this same chapter, Jesus says: "There will be more rejoicing in heaven over one sinner who repents than over ninety-nine righteous persons who do not need to repent." This sets the tone for the entire chapter. The prodigal son asks his father for his inheritance and then goes off to a distant land and lives a debauched life. A famine then hits that land and he falls into need. He finally ends up working with pigs and is so desperate that he desires to eat the pig food. It is at this stage that he comes to his senses and decides to return to his father. A cynic might conclude

that he has only come to his senses to return to his father because he is desperate. The account informs us that he does not expect to be welcomed back as a son, but would be happy if his father simply allowed him to be a hired hand. What sort of reception does he receive?

10. "While he was still a long way off, his father saw him and was filled with compassion for him; he ran to his son, threw his arms around him and kissed him. The son said to him, 'Father, I have sinned against heaven and against you. I am no longer worthy to be called your son.' But the father said to his servants, 'Quick! Bring the best robe and put it on him. Put a ring on his finger and sandals on his feet. Bring the fattened calf and kill it. Let's have a feast and celebrate. For this son of mine was dead and is alive again; he was lost and is found.' So they began to celebrate." (Luke 15:20-24). We now see clearly how inappropriate a reinstatement hearing would be if we are to truly be guided by Jesus' powerful illustration. Why would imperfect humans need to question the motives of an individual who has come to his senses and wants to present himself to God once more? In the last study article we talked about surprises, and this story contains such a surprise. The son was probably worried about whether his father would accept him at all, but to his utter surprise the father showered him in love and all manner of gifts and privileges. Bearing in mind the joy that is taking place in heaven at the moment when a person repents, we

would be acting like the brother of the prodigal son if we in any way resented him being completely welcomed back; it is a time for rejoicing; a celebration.

11. In recent years we have seen a move in a positive direction in this regard. For example, in the past when an announcement was made to say that an individual had been reinstated in the congregation, it was considered inappropriate for there to be applause for such an announcement. This clearly gave the impression that there was still some shame to be carried by the returning one and his or her return was more of a solemn warning than a reason for joy. Then we decided a few years ago that there may well be spontaneous, dignified applause when such an announcement is made. While this was a step in the right direction, dignified applause does not match the description of the celebration organised by the father of the prodigal son. We have even produced video presentations that show a recently reinstated sister feeling extremely distressed over her past sin and wondering whether she has really been forgiven. In that video we shamefully portrayed her own family giving her a very cool welcome after an absence in their lives of 15 years. No wonder she felt distressed!

12. That video has been deleted and will never be used again in the future. We can only apologise for any distress that such a video might have caused. One of the most harmful aspects of that video presentation was the way the daughter was seen to say that if her

family had so much as answered the telephone to her, she might never have felt the need to return to Jehovah. So many people were appalled by this blatant emotional blackmail and correctly pointed out that the mother, acting in obedience to the direction of the organisation, was ignoring not only her natural affection for a daughter, but was being forced to act against common human interest and fellow feeling; for all the mother might have known, the daughter may have been calling to say she had just been in a car accident, or was so depressed by the situation she found herself in that she was considering suicide.

13. So, what is the arrangement now for those who commit sins? And what can those do who are at this time in a disfellowshipped state? The final passage of scripture that we are going to consider is one that has been misapplied in the past. Please turn to James chapter 5 and we shall read verses 14 and 15: "Is anyone among you in trouble? Let them call the elders... to pray over them and anoint them with oil in the name of the Lord. And the prayer offered in faith will make the sick person well; the Lord will raise him up." We often stop the reading there and assume that these verses have been talking about someone who is spiritually sick and who must call the elders to make confession of a sin and allow the elders to decide whether he or she is sufficiently repentant to have their sins forgiven. The very last line of verse 15 indicates that this is not what the preceding words are talking

about: "**If** they have committed sins, they **will** be forgiven."

14. As we saw when we discussed the verses in 1st Corinthians chapter 5, the ceasing of fellowship with a person was only to take place in the extreme case of someone claiming to be a brother or sister who was continuing in a course of sin, a person referred to in the same chapter as 'a wicked person' (1st Corinthian 5:13). Someone who confesses his or her sins and wants to change could hardly be thought of as a wicked person. In fact, as this verse in James clearly shows, a person who calls the elders and asks for help will be assured that his sins will be forgiven. That is what the ransom sacrifice of Jesus has made possible. There is nowhere in the Christian scriptures where we read that members of a congregation can only gain forgiveness for their sins by going to the elders. The very next verse in James chapter 5 highlights that all in the congregation can hear the confession of a fellow brother or sister: "Therefore confess your sins to each other and pray for each other so that you may be healed. The prayer of the righteous person is powerful and effective." (James 5:16).

15. So what can those currently referred to as disfellowshipped expect if they return to the meetings? Hopefully something far more than dignified applause; it will not be unusual for a meeting to be interrupted for a considerable time if the doors swing open and such a person walks in. The interruption will be caused by a

swarm of people offering hugs and kisses, reflecting the joy that is taking place in heaven. In fact, there will be nothing wrong with the meeting being cancelled and the entire gathering reconvening at a pub or restaurant for a celebration. Then truly, Jesus' words will find fulfilment: "Come to me, all you who are weary and burdened, and I will give you rest." On the other hand, if disfellowshipped ones do not want to return to meetings, then they are not claiming to be a brother or sister and should be treated as Jesus treated all the people he met - with love and kindness.

16. In an environment of love and forgiveness there will indeed be great refreshment. Arrangements in the past created a culture of fear and in some cases dishonesty. Those loaded down were often too scared to tell anyone about their errors and slip-ups because they feared the judgment of a judicial committee. Some disfellowshipped ones tried returning to the congregation, but after sitting in a few meetings with everyone ignoring them, they gave up and felt isolated and desolate. Some of them never saw their family members again. Many have killed themselves...

And the writing just stopped there. The brother assigned to write this particular article got up from where he was sitting and walked away.

Printed in Great Britain
by Amazon